DINGO HUNTING

A SHORT STORY

ALEXANDRIA BLAELOCK

BlueMere Books
MELBOURNE, AUSTRALIA

For permission requests, please contact enquiries@bluemerebooks.com.

Ordering Information:
Discounts are available on quantity purchases. For details, contact orders@bluemerebooks.com.

Dingo Hunting/Alexandria Blaelock
paperback ISBN: 978-1-922744-43-2
digital ISBN: 978-1-922744-44-9

Book Layout © BookDesignTemplates.com
Cover Art © grandfailure/Depositphotos

DINGO HUNTING

Steve led the way up the embankment, because, well, Steve always did.

Something about his wild blond surfer hair (hundreds of kilometres from the sea) and his deep ocean blue eyes just inspired the others to follow him regardless of the consequences.

That was how Jimmy lost a finger in the combine harvester accident, though you can't really say it was an accident when we all knew the risks.

Jimmy just wasn't fast enough that time.

We called it the embankment, but it was a natural phenomenon. We had no idea whether it was an ancient caldera, cenote or maybe even a meteor strike.

But there was a steep climb up, followed by a quick, squealing stumble down through the red dirt, and you were in the perfect place for teenage hijinks.

The basin was so large you almost couldn't see the other side of it. The slopes were covered in a sparse layer of scrub that thickened as you reached the bottom, so you had to fight your way into the centre of the depression.

The bushes were dry and scratchy, and one time Scarlet cut her shoulder open and needed twenty-five stitches to close it back up.

So, every now and then we'd borrow a couple of chainsaws and hack a winding path through to the centre.

For some reason, we thought a winding path would be less obvious to outsiders than a straight one.

And it did make arriving at the centre seem much more like a journey.

The centre held a mysterious stone circle that needed a particular kind of approach, and a nice straight, broad avenue just wasn't the way to do it.

The circle wasn't like a Stonehenge kind circle, all nice and neat and precise.

It was just a bunch of large rocks, but when you looked at them from the right angle, they looked exactly like a circle of snarling dingo teeth rising from the ground.

Like some monstrous beast had been caught just before it manifested and was now stuck forever with just its snout poking out of the ground.

And when the wind came in from just the right direction, you could almost believe it was whining and begging to be set free.

And of course, the path we made was as if you'd walked up its throat and out its mouth, so it seemed like you'd crossed a mystical portal into another world.

Naturally, best at night in the flickering light of a fire made with collected scrub branches.

And even better with a few stolen beers and a couple of joints.

The place had always inspired rumours about lost and stolen children - the kids who were too slow to get away from the faeries, but what modern kid believes in them anymore?

Especially in the outback of Australia.

When faeries remained back in assorted old countries, and anyway, they couldn't survive in the bright, direct, desert sunlight, could they?

Never did we think there was any truth to those rumours.

If, in fact, there were any missing kids at all, we thought they'd just packed up their swag and run off to the big smoke.

Like we all wanted to.

Though maybe only Steve really did, while we just said we did for bravado's sake.

So.

Steve had a thing for pretty, dark-haired Katie, and we all knew she didn't really like him at all.

But kids are kids, and Steve was Steve, and Katie didn't really have a choice in the matter.

Katie belonged to Steve for as long as he wanted her, and when it got difficult, we just kind of slunk away so we wouldn't be tempted to do anything stupid.

Poor Katie.

That night, Steve paused at the top of the embankment for a moment, silhouetted by the full moon before rushing down the other side.

Someone else had got there first.

We could see the glow of their fire, smell their barbecued meat and hear their deep drunken laughter.

Steve was ropable, and we all kind of stepped back out of his way while he told us what he was going to do with the intruders, and how we were going to help.

Steve talked a good game, but we were kids, and they sounded like men, and most likely, we didn't have a hope in hell of doing what Steve wanted.

So while Steve delivered a rousing and inciting speech to his assembled troops, most of them took the opportunity to do a runner before things kicked off.

I didn't have any intention of getting involved, but this time, I was the one not fast enough.

He collared me and pushed me ahead of the rest, so I stumbled out the dingo's jaws into a roar of grown-up laughter.

They were tall, well-built guys with longish black hair. But they looked like bad guys to me, leather pants and tatts and stuff, like a bikie gang.

The leader's dark pants were tucked into his long boots, and his scratched and scarred, dark leather vest hung loose and open.

His bare chest and arms were covered in tattoos, and in the flames, they seemed to writhe across his body in torment.

His black eyes were outlined in Kohl, and as his gaze glanced off me, I was so afraid I tripped over my feet and wet my keks as I fell.

I slithered the hell out of the way as fast as I could.

He rested his hands low on his hips as he cocked his head to look Steve up and down. Katie was a step behind Steve, and he was holding her by the wrist so she couldn't get away.

The leader smiled a little as he walked around the pair.

Steve kind of leant away from him, and Katie kind of leaned towards him.

The fire cast his face into light and shade, outlining his hook nose and glinting off the silver crown-like thing that held his top knot in place.

He pulled Katie towards him, and I don't know if Steve was surprised or recognised a superior force, but he let go of her.

The guy spread his legs a little and pushed his hands up under her skirt. He cupped her under the bum as he held her close, pressed his face into the crook of her neck, and breathed in deeply.

Then he kind of growled, bent her backwards and forced a kiss on her lips.

A long, slow, deep, thorough kiss.

I thought Steve'd go mental, but he took a step back, away from the pair.

"I'll let you go if you leave her behind," the guy said.

Steve turned, and without a word, ran back down the dingo's throat.

I danced around a bit, backwards and forwards, half a mind to do the same.

But I wasn't going to leave Katie there on her own, so I darted forwards and punched the guy in the back.

He laughed.

I got a bit mad and went for him again, but he turned and flicked me in the middle of my forehead with his middle finger like I was a bug on his shoulder and I don't remember anything after that.

《《 • 》》

The next morning, when Katie woke me up, I was still inside the embankment, but there was no sign of the bikies.

I had the mother of all hangovers.

She helped me up, draped me over her shoulder and helped me scramble over the embankment.

"What happened?" I asked.

"What do you remember?"

I wasn't above a bit of exaggeration, "nothing after that guy hit me."

"What guy?"

"You know, the bikie guy."

"There wasn't a guy. We just got drunk and told scary stories."

"Well, where are all the others then?"

"You wandered off and got lost. I got worried and came back early for you."

I didn't point out any of the holes in her story, like the adult size boot prints.

Or the chewed-up bones.

Or that she was wearing the same clothes, and they were filthy

Or what I later found out was a fingernail-sized bruise on my forehead.

When I got home, I was in so much trouble I was grounded for a month, and my parents set me to fencing, checking and maintaining the pumps, pipes and dam banks, and cleaning out the milking sheds and machinery.

When the cops came round asking after Steve, I wanted to protect Katie, so I told them her story.

That I got drunk and passed out early.

He was there at the start, and he was gone when I work up.

I didn't mention the bikie gang.

I saw Katie and the others at Church, but no one knew where he was.

We agreed he must have packed up and run away to Melbourne.

Doubt anyone else believed it either, but without a body, what were the other options?

We never went back to the embankment.

The years went by, and Steve's folks sold up the farm and moved away.

His missing-persons poster faded and went brown, the edges curled up in the heat, and he was forgotten.

Katie went away to study graphic design, and I took over the farm when my parents moved to the seaside.

It was like Steve had never even existed, except, maybe, as a scary story for the next generation to take over the embankment.

After a bit, Katie's Mum got sick, and she came home to take care of things.

She had an online business with customers all over the place and said it didn't make any difference to her whether she worked from home or the City.

We hooked up.

One night, as she reached over to haul herself out of bed, I noticed a burn on her left shoulder blade.

Something about the way she moved made it look like a dingo howling.

When I asked her about it, she tried to pretend it wasn't there.

And after I traced its outline on her back, that it was something else.

But I reminded her I was the last one there the night Steve disappeared.

She looked over her shoulder at me, shaking her head a little so her long black hair fell back and concealed the mark.

I reached out to brush it aside so I could inspect the mark closely, but something in her eyes made me put my hand back down.

She looked at me for a long time, then got up, pulled her hair aside and placed herself in front of the mirror where she could see the dingo clearly.

It was all done so smoothly it was clear she'd done it a billion times before.

She reached behind her back and touched the mark.

From where I lay, it looked like she was stroking its chin.

"I made a deal," she said.

The moon went behind a cloud, casting her face into shadow, but I swear the dingo on her back yawned, and a faint red glow rose in her eyes.

And then the moon came out, and she threw herself back on the bed beside me, leaning on an elbow, absently stroking my chest as she thought about what to say.

"Most men think the pack leader is the alpha male, but they're wrong," she smiled down at me, one of her canines caught on her lip.

"The leader is the alpha female. It's only by her leave that her lieutenant decides what to hunt, where to eat, when to sleep and mate with her.

"And clearly, the best leader is young, strong and determined."

She was looking past me, out the window, towards the embankment in the distance.

"Someone cunning, who can control the worst tendencies of the pack, and drive them down the path they need to go."

She flicked one of my nipples with her middle finger, and I gasped, unsure whether to cover it or tough it out.

"She's the mother of the pack. Dogs learn their places while they're at her teats. Those with a fighting spirit take their places at front and scout the way, others wait their turn and protect the rear. But they all obey their mother.

"Sometimes, a pack loses its mother. They'll carry on for a time, but without a new mother, they're lost, without direction. Sometimes, a pack like that tears itself apart.

"And when we met that pack on the embankment, I realised it was missing its mother."

"But they weren't dogs, they were bikies."

"Were they? What gives you that idea?"

"Well, they were big hairy guys in leather."

"Were they?"

"Well, maybe they weren't bikies, but they were definitely guys."

"Are you sure?"

"Okay, I wasn't conscious for long, but they sure looked like guys."

"They did look like guys, but they were elemental dingoes, in the form of humans."

I thought she was making fun of me, so I leaned towards her, intending to sit up and get out of bed in a huff.

She laid her palm on my chest, and no matter how hard I tried, I wasn't strong enough to sit up past that point.

"I thought you wanted to hear the story."

"I wanted the truth, and in this day and age that doesn't include spirit creatures."

She smiled and moved her hand.

I was still straining to sit up, so I rocketed up, through the place where she'd been sitting and fell on the floor.

Hard.

I looked around for her, and she was on the other side of the room, half-dressed already.

"Katie, what's going on?"

She paused as she pulled on her t-shirt, "There are more things in heaven and earth, Horatio, than are dreamt of in your philosophy." she quoted.

"But Katie—"

"Call me when you really want to know."

She walked out the door, and by the time I'd disentangled myself from the sheets and run, naked, out to the verandah, she was gone.

No sign that she'd even been there, save maybe, for a drift of dust in the light breeze.

《《 • 》》

So she'd got my goat up with that bloody dog story, though given her Mum was a breeder she'd know all that stuff.

But elementals for god's sake.

She'd be telling me the bikie gang were weredingoes next.

I stamped about the farm, milking cows, and getting more and more annoyed as the days went by.

And then, I don't know why, but I started watching the animals.

The milking herd follows a clear daily routine in and out of the milking sheds twice a day, but I noticed it was the same old cow that got the herd moving.

We don't use many dogs, because it's in a cow's best interest to get into the milking shed, but I noticed my bitch Blue yipping at the others, keeping the pack in line.

Was there a nugget of truth in the elemental story?

I decided to visit the embankment.

And I was a little afraid, so I took Blue with me.

I parked the ute in the flat space by the road we used to park our pushbikes, though threw them is a more accurate description.

Blue leapt out of the tray almost before I'd pulled the handbrake, and was off up the rise before I'd got one foot on the ground.

I confess I dithered, afraid both of what I might find, and what I might not.

The scrub was wild enough that I thought no one had visited for years, but the town's dying what with the drought and low milk prices.

I pushed my way further and further in, and all of a sudden, I broke into the centre.

Only it wasn't the centre, the stone circle was missing, and I was looking up at the other side.

So, I climbed up and looked back across the basin, and all I could see was dense bush.

No paths, no stones, no gaps.

Blue yipped from somewhere, and I whistled, and in a few seconds, she came bounding up the rise to meet me.

So that was that.

I called Katie.

《《 • 》》

It was a hot day, a few days after her mother's funeral, when we met at the local footy ground.

I went to kiss her, but she twisted out of my grasp.

And I guess that was fair enough.

"I'm sorry about your Mum Katie."

She grimaced, "what do you want Mike?"

"I went to the embankment, and the stones are gone."

"So?"

"I want to know about the elementals."

She rolled her eyes at me, "It was just a story, I was winding you up."

"I don't believe you."

She shrugged and turned away as if she was looking for someone "not my problem."

I could see through the armhole of her tank top, and I thought maybe the dingo scar was gone from her shoulder.

I wondered for a moment if I'd imagined the whole thing.

She waved at a guy who walked onto the pitch.

"I've got to go Mike," she said, "I'm leaving town today, and my lift's just arrived."

He was a tall, well-built guy with short black hair. His blue button-down shirt was tucked into his jeans, but the sleeves were rolled up to his forearms.

When he saw her, he opened his arms, and as his sleeves pulled up, I thought I saw the flash of coloured tatts.

She jogged across to him, leaping the last step into his embrace.

He swung her around, and I thought I recognised his hook-nosed profile from somewhere but I couldn't say where.

That was the last time I saw Katie.

But now and again, when I hear a wild dog, or maybe a dingo howling, or see one silhouetted on the horizon, I wonder if it's her.

THE END

ABOUT THE AUTHOR

Alexandria Blaelock writes stories, some of them for *Ellery Queen's Mystery Magazine* and *Pulphouse Fiction Magazine*.

She's also written five self-help books applying business techniques to personal matters like getting dressed, cleaning house, and feeding your friends.

Discover more at www.alexandriablaelock.com.

BOOKS BY
ALEXANDRIA BLAELOCK

SHORT STORY COLLECTIONS

The Histories of Hayward Hall
Lovelorn, Lovestruck and Love at First Sight
Common or Garden Variety Heroes
Case Files of the Wilkinson Detective Agency
Unavoidable Fates
Christmas Travesties
Five Faces of Felicia Clarke

OTHER FICTION

That Love Nonsense
Taipan vs Brown

MS BLAELOCK'S BOOKS

Stress Free Dinner Parties
Signature Wardrobe Planning
Holistic Personal Finance
Minimally Viable Housekeeping
Planning a Life Worth Living

SELECTED SHORT STORIES

Alma's Grace
Balancing the Book
Carmelita Basingstoke
Fate in Your Hands
Kiss of Death
Lady of the Looking Glass
Life in the Security Directorate
Long Weekend in the Snow
Love in the Past Tense
Love in the Security Directorate
Morning Star, Evening Star, Superstar
Needy Bitch
Payton's Run
Phoenix Child
Secret Singer
Shining Star
Ship in a Bottle
Simone Says Hands in the Air
Special Relativity in Space
The Bygone Boyfriend
The Day the Schedule Broke
The Ghost Detectors
The Guardian's Vigil
The Mince Pie Mystery
The Mystery of the Master Suite
The Pseudonym's Bride
The Shadow Thieves
The Space-Time Paradox
Toy Soldiers